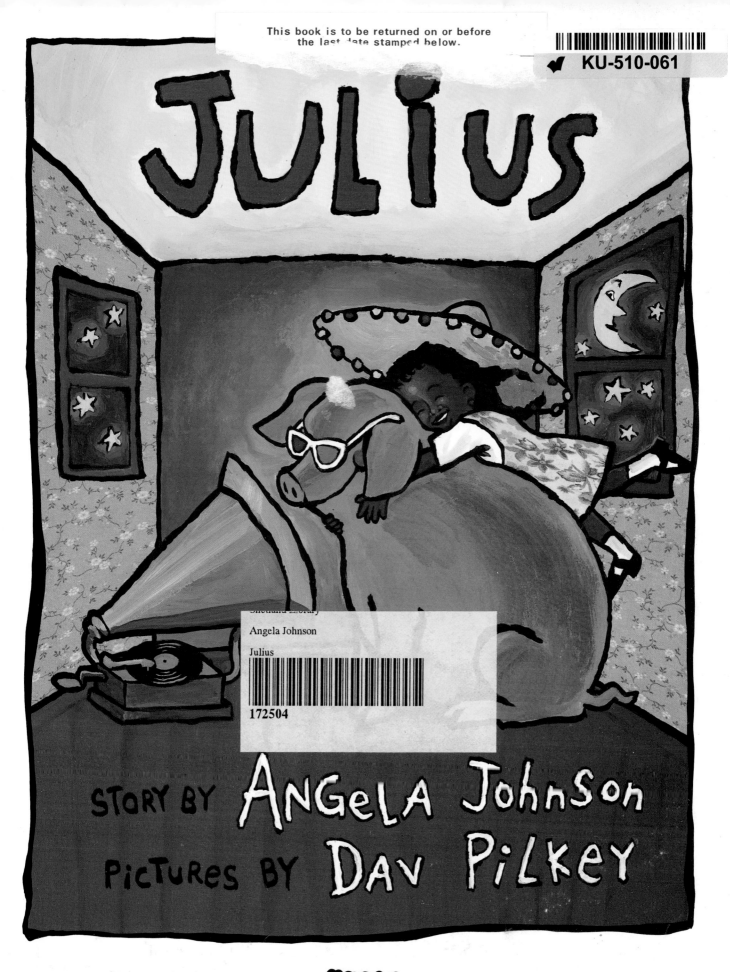

JULIUS

STORY BY ANGELA JOHNSON
PICTURES BY DAV PILKEY

SHETLAND LIBRARY
ORCHARD BOOKS

ORCHARD BOOKS
96 Leonard Street, London EC2A 4RH
Orchard Books Australia
14 Mars Road, Lane Cove, NSW 2066
1 85213 943 9 (hardback)
1 85213 862 9 (paperback)
First published by Orchard Books, USA, 1993
First published in Great Britain 1995
First paperback publication 1995
Text copyright © 1993 by Angela Johnson
Illustrations copyright © 1993 by Dav Pilkey
A CIP catalogue record for this book is available from the British Library.
Printed in Belgium

To Ashley,
who loves the music too

Maya's grandaddy lived in Alabama,
but spent the winter in Alaska.

He told Maya that was the reason he
liked ice cubes in his coffee.

On one of Grandaddy's visits from
Alaska, he brought a crate.
   A surprise for Maya!
   "Something that will teach you fun
and sharing." Grandaddy smiled.
"Something for my special you."

Maya hoped it was a horse or an older
brother.
She'd always wanted one or the other.

But it was a pig.

A big pig.
An Alaskan pig, who did a polar bear
imitation and climbed out of the crate.

Julius had come.

Maya's parents didn't think that they
would like Julius.
He showed them no fun, no sharing.

Maya loved Julius, though, so he stayed.

There never was enough food in the
house after Julius came to stay.
He slurped coffee and ate too much
peanut butter.

He would roll himself in flour when
he wanted Maya to bake him biscuits.

Julius made lots of mess and spread the newspaper everywhere before anyone could read it.

He left crumbs on the sheets and
never picked up his towels.

Julius made too much noise.
He'd stay up late watching old films,

and he'd always play records when everybody else wanted to read.

But Maya knew the other Julius too...

The Julius who was fun to take on walks because he did great dog imitations and chased cats.

The Julius who sneaked into shops
with her and tried on clothes.
Julius liked anything blue and stretchy.

They'd try on hats too.
Maya liked red felt.
Julius liked straw—it tasted better.

Trying on shoes was hard, though...

Julius would swing for hours in
the playground with Maya.

He'd protect her from the scary things
at night too...sometimes.

**Maya loved the Julius who taught her
how to dance to jazz records...**

and eat peanut butter from the jar,
without getting any on the ceiling.
Maya didn't think all the older brothers
in the world could have taught her that.

Julius loved the Maya who taught him
that even though he was a pig he didn't
have to act like he lived in a barn.

Julius didn't think all the Alaskan pigs
in the world could have taught him that.

**Maya shared the things she'd learned
from Julius with her friends.
Swinging…**

trying on hats, and dancing to jazz records.

Julius shared the things Maya had taught
him with her parents...sometimes.

And that was all right, because living
with Maya and sharing everything
was even better than being a cool pig
from Alaska.